Heroes to the Rescue

Published by arrangement with Entertainment One and Ladybird Books, A Penguin Company.

This book is based on the TV series *Ben and Holly's Little Kingdom*. *Ben and Holly's Little Kingdom* is created by Neville Astley and Mark Baker.

Ben and Holly's Little Kingdom © The Elf Factory Ltd/Entertainment One UK Ltd 2008

ISBN 978-1-338-23032-1

10 9 8 7 6 5 4 3 2 1   18 19 20 21 22
Printed in the U.S.A.   40

First printing 2018
Book design by Carla Alpert

The Elf Factory

SCHOLASTIC INC.

Holly and her friends are playing in the meadow when Ben appears in a funny costume. "Hi, Ben!" they call out.

"I'm not Ben," Ben replies. "Ben is my regular name. When I put on my superhero costume, I become Elf Man!"

"I'll be Fairy Girl!" says Holly. She magicks herself a costume. Jake is Captain Crazy, and Barnaby is the Strongest Boy in the World.

"What about me?" asks Strawberry.

"We can't all be goodies," says Ben. "Someone has to be the supervillain!"

"Okay! I will be Strawberry Ice Queen," says Strawberry. "I'm going to take over the Little Kingdom, and you must try to stop me!"

"It's Elf Man and Fairy Girl against Strawberry Ice Queen and her gang!" says Ben. "To the Elfmobile, Fairy Girl!"

"Do your worst, Ice Queen!" Holly shouts as they fly away on Gaston.

They are going to the Elf Cave.

Inside the Elf Cave, Ben has made a secret hideout. Suddenly, Strawberry appears on Ben's computer.

"I am the Ice Queen, and I'm going to make everything freezy and cold!" Strawberry declares. "Muahahaha!"

"Uh-oh," says Holly. "What are we going to do now?"

On the other side of the Little Kingdom, Strawberry is with her gang of supervillains in front of the Great Elf Tree. She waves her magic wand, and soon the entire Little Kingdom is cold and covered in snow.

The grown-up elves are very confused.

"Snow in July?" says Mrs. Elf.

"Look!" says Mr. Elf, pointing to the edge of the Little Kingdom. "The snow stops here."

"This is ridiculous!" says the Wise Old Elf with a frown. "I'll bet my beard Nanny Plum has something to do with this. Let's go see her."

They find Nanny Plum, and the Wise Old Elf tells her she must stop the snow.

"It's not my fault!" says Nanny Plum. "Maybe it's the work of a supervillain!"

"Nonsense!" says the Wise Old Elf.
"Supervillains and superheroes don't exist."
"Then what's that?" asks Nanny Plum, pointing
to a symbol lighting up the sky.

Ben is making the symbol from inside the Elf Cave.

"When people need our help, they'll be able to find us by following this symbol," he says to Holly.

Just then, there's a knock at the door.

Gaston

"We need your help!" calls Mr. Elf from outside. "The whole Little Kingdom is covered in snow!"

"That's the work of the Ice Queen!" says Holly. "Leave it to Elf Man and Fairy Girl. We'll take care of it!"

Ben and Holly fly around the Little Kingdom until they find Strawberry Ice Queen's secret hideout: a huge, sparkling palace made entirely out of ice.

"We've come to stop you, Ice Queen!" they shout.

"Muahaha!" laughs the Ice Queen. "You'll never stop me!"

"But the grown-ups are a little bit upset about all of this freezing snow," says Holly.

"Oops," says Strawberry. "Are we in trouble?"

"I don't think so, as long as the game is over," says Ben.
"Okay!" says Strawberry. "I'll make everything melt away."

The sun comes out and the Little Kingdom is warm again.

"We're saved!" cheers the Wise Old Elf. "Thanks to Elf Man and Fairy Girl."

"If only we knew their secret identities . . ." says Mr. Elf. But of course they never will!